CHRISTMAS HOPE DEFERRED

AN AMISH CHRISTMAS ROMANCE

Naomi Troyer

Contents

Chapter 1
The Mahogany Clock

Edith Lapp slid the pork roast, thickly rubbed with brown sugar and fresh herbs, into the oven and shut the door, her mouth already watering in anticipation. A sharp rat-tat-tat at the front door of her parents' home caught her attention, and she dropped the oven mitts on the table, instinctively rushing to get to the door first, even though there was nobody with her in the house.

She knew that rat-tat-tat so well, it may as well have beat in time with the rhythm of her heart. Flinging the door open, she gazed into the beloved face she had known she would see.

"Sy! You're early!" she exclaimed, joy radiating from her face and eyes.

Instead of the usual beaming grin she got in return, Silas Hauptfleisch looked nervous. He smiled sheepishly. "Hullo, Edie," he said, his eyes already scanning the interior of the living room as he stepped over the threshold.

Edith closed the door behind him, her insides quivering with a sense of anticipation considerably less exhilarating than the one she had just felt in the kitchen. She couldn't imagine what could be the matter. Had there been trouble at home? Where were his parents? He had said nothing about coming alone. Add to that, he really had arrived very early.

"You're alone?" he asked, taking off his gloves and wringing his hands by the gas heater.

"I am," Edith replied, probing his face with her eyes. "Maem is delivering some meal packages to the poor and Daed had one last furniture delivery to make. Hess is picking up some more candles and greenery for us. She took Caleb with her." Her heart was quivering now. Why did he look so serious? Even a little frightened?

"Okay," Silas said, sounding as if he were about to take on an army of Englisch. He hung up his hat, coat, and scarf and fiddled with his suspenders. Edith watched him, feeling as nervous as he looked.

"Is something the matter, Sy?" she asked him querulously. He spun around to look at her with startled eyes and then shook his head.

"Ney, all is gut," he tried to assure her, his face telling her a different story to his words. "This is for you."

He held out a parcel wrapped in brown paper.

"Oh, danke, Sy!" Edith exclaimed, taking it from his hands. She hesitated. "Your gift is upstairs in my room," she added shyly.

Silas shook his head, his face still mysteriously serious. "Never mind. You can give it to me later," he said. "Open yours first."

Edith nodded, deciding to trust him. They had known each other since they were small children and he had never withheld any kind of important information from her unless there was a good reason for it. She smiled, relaxing a little into her choice to have faith in him.

Placing the parcel on the coffee table, she knelt down and ripped off the paper. As the brown covering fell away, Edith gasped. It was the most beautiful mantel clock she had ever seen.

The wood was a rich mahogany, shaped into a sturdy box with a glass door and topped with three tiers of beveled wood and a brass handle. The face was polished brass with pitch black Roman numerals showing the hours, and a rich filigree of brass decorating the corners.

Edith looked up into Silas's earnest gaze, her heart rejoicing as she thought of the significance of a clock as a gift, especially one this beautiful. More especially one that she had pointed out one day when they were wandering about town and passed Daniel King's clock shop quite by accident, or so she had thought.

Silas swallowed, the intensity on his face deepening. "Edith," he said, his voice gravelly as he uncharacteristically used her full name. "I want to spend all my hours with you, for the rest of our lives."

Edith felt as if a thousand butterflies had been let loose in her stomach. She sprang to her feet, tears of joy already spilling over her cheeks. She had known this was coming, known it for a long, long time, and yet the long time of knowing did nothing to reduce the explosion of happiness that erupted inside her.

"Me too!" she exclaimed, throwing her arms around Silas' neck and lifting her feet into the air as he wrapped his arms around her and they spun round and around, laughing with a mixture of relief and happiness. At last Silas set her down on the couch and settled himself in beside her.

"Here, help me wind it up," he said, drawing the clock nearer to the sofa they sat on. Opening the door, he took out the windup key and handed it to Edith. Then he held the clock on his lap for her to insert the key and wind up the dormant springs of the clock.

Turning the metal key, she listened to the rich tick-tock rhythm sounding and felt a thrill run through her. Every moment she would be with him, the only man she had ever loved, until their beautiful clock ticked away the last second of her life. Nothing could have made her happier.

Silas set the time to her parents' clock hanging on the living room wall. Then he took her hand and looked deeply into her eyes.

"Gott has been good to me, my love," he told her. "All my life I've known you would be my wife and all my life the only woman I've ever wanted was you, since the moment I took that sticky schnecken from your chubby five-year-old fingers as a boy of barely seven."

Before Edith could respond, the front door flew open and Edith's younger sister and brother burst into the room, their arms laden with green boughs and large candles. Hess stopped in her tracks, her eyes growing wide as they settled on the mahogany clock.

"Maem! Daed!" she called over her shoulder. "Silas did it!"

Edith laughed again, collapsing into Silas's arms while his own warm, deep-throated laughter harmonized with hers.

"I smell pork roasting," Caleb remarked, wrinkling his nose and sniffing appreciatively.

"Caleb!" their father reprimanded him as he stepped over the threshold. "Your sister just got betrothed after years of us wondering when Silas was going to pop the question and all you can think about is food?"

More laughter filled the room, followed by ecstatic hugs and kisses all round, while Edith retold the story of how Silas had proposed. Then the happy little family fell to making the final preparations for the Christmas feast. There would be neighbors coming over soon, and they still had much to do. As they worked, Edith thought about their guests.

Most of them would be the Lapp and Hauptfleisch extended family, some would be friends and neighbors, some would even be Englisch from nearby farms who had befriended her family. She wondered how many would notice the new clock still ticking away on the coffee table in the living room, and how many would know what it signified.

One thing she knew for sure, all would celebrate with her and her Silas on the new phase of life they were about to step into, when the time came for the announcement a few weeks before the wedding.

Thank You, Gott. I couldn't have asked for a better Christmas, she thought contentedly. *Now my life is perfect and I know I will never be unhappy again.* It was a sweet, sweet feeling. One she hoped would last forever.

Chapter 2
A Bump in the Road

Christmas flew by, followed by New Year, with all the usual feasting and games and visiting back and forth between the religious observances. The other young members of their community cast furtive glances at Edith and Silas at the singings throughout the year.

Edith knew it was clear there was a new energy between them. But Edith had made Hess and Caleb swear they wouldn't tell a soul about the wedding plans until it was time for the happy couple to do so themselves, and she knew her parents would keep mum about it.

So their secret went undetected, as much as the gossips might conjecture about how the way they looked at each other was just a bit different from before. Anyone visiting the Lapp household late in the evening, though, would be left with no doubts what was afoot.

"Well, I honestly don't know if that's a good idea, dochder," Aaron Lapp said dubiously, poring over the notebook that Edith had placed before him on the dining table. "If you're planning a Christmas wedding, we'll have to have store-bought celery and who knows what the quality will be like in that case."

"Ach, Daed," Edith sighed. "Silas and I have dreamed of a Christmas wedding for years. We can't let something as silly as traditional table decorations get in the way of that."

Aaron tut-tutted and shook his head. "The young of today, you have your own ideas about everything."

"Ach, ney, Daed," Edith replied laughingly, noticing the familiar twinkle of mischief in her father's eye. "Sy and I are far beyond rumspringa years. Besides, aren't you the one who always tells me, 'If you aim at nothing, you're bound to hit it?'"

"Then I have tripped myself up with my own words," Aaron lamented with mock despair. Edith laughed and hugged her father.

"I can't wait to announce this wedding at last!" Abigail Lapp declared, walking through from the kitchen, wiping her hands dry on her apron. "I hear Betty Weaver makes the best roasht in the county and I'll need a couple of months to butter her up enough for her to give me the recipe. With all the secret keeping about the engagement, I couldn't dare risk mentioning it sooner."

"You're making the roasht yourself?" her husband interjected.

"For my oldest dochder's wedding? Of course, mei mann," Abigail laughed, kissing him on the forehead as she swept by.

"Maem, when exactly were you thinking of making the announcement?" Edith queried, aware that her mother might have plans Edith didn't know about yet.

"Why, this Sunday at worship, of course," Abigail shot over her shoulder as she headed for the washroom.

"But Maem! Sy and I …" she trailed off, aware that her mother wasn't listening anymore.

"Just let her do it, liebchen," Aaron advised his daughter. "I know you wanted to hold off another week, but it will be a full two weeks before the next Sunday service, and I don't think she'll be able to last that long before she bursts." He smiled warmly and patted Edith's hand.

Edith smiled back. "Okay, Daed," she relented. "As long as Maem promises to bake her famous raisin pies. We all know how Sy loves those, and it would be a shame if he can't have them at his own wedding."

Abigail appeared in the doorway as if by magic. "Raisin pies? You mean *funeral pies*! Why would you want something like that at a wedding?"

"Ach, Maem, nobody bothers with things like that anymore," Edith protested. "And I said I'd let you make the announcement this week, so you have to give me something in return."

Abigail's face creased into a smile. "Of course I'll make you funeral pies for your wedding, mei lieve," she quipped, crossing over to her husband and daughter and placing an arm around the former's shoulders. "You and me, Aaron, we're just getting old, that's all it is," she said with an exaggerated sigh.

"That's the bitter with the sweet, mei fraa," Aaron reminded her. "If we weren't getting older, our daughter would not be getting married." He beamed at Edith proudly.

"Jah, you are right, as usual, mei mann," Abigail agreed, turning a smiling face to her daughter. "We are happy for you, Edith, so thrilled."

Edith felt herself relax, only then noticing that they had tensed her up. "It feels too good to be true, to be honest," she said, feeling suddenly melancholy, an emotion totally opposite to what she knew she should be feeling. "I keep expecting something to go wrong."

"There's no reason to expect such things," Abigail assured her. "You and Silas have done everything by the Ordnung and by the word of Gott. Why should anything go wrong?"

"Ah, isn't that what Job must have been thinking the day before his testing?" Aaron chimed in sagely.

"Don't go stirring the pot, now, Aaron Lapp," his wife chastised him, but his words were already burned deep in Edith's mind. Her father was right. She knew there was nothing anybody could do to earn the favor of God. He gave it freely when He knew the time was right and when it fulfilled His purposes.

Through the strange sense of foreboding that seemed to follow her around like a shadow, she trusted Him. *You know the future already, Gott,* she prayed silently that night while she lay in bed, waiting for sleep. *Bishop Beiler often says that Your ways are higher than our ways and Your thoughts far above ours. Sy and I cannot claim anything from You because of our good behavior. We can only trust that You will make sure Your purposes are realized in our lives, no matter what.*

It was a few days after her parents' beaming, if formal announcement of their daughter's upcoming wedding to Silas Hauptfleisch, that the pains started.

At first, she thought she had eaten something bad, but they continued for the rest of the following week. Sometimes they were terrible, other times it was just an incessant feeling of heartburn and indigestion. In the weeks that followed, into late November, her discomfort grew steadily worse, and her appetite dwindled to almost nothing.

"My dresses don't fit me anymore, Maem," she said one morning as she dragged herself to the breakfast table and looked around at the food that usually would have had her dishing up a second helping. Now she could barely stomach the idea of swallowing even a spoonful.

"I've noticed that, liebchen," Abigail agreed, deep concern etched in her eyes. "We'll have to go back to Dr. Neumann. The medication he gave you clearly isn't working, and if we have to take in your wedding dress one more time, we may as well just make an entire new one."

"The medicine helps a little," Edith came to the doctor's defense. Her mother gave her a sorrowful look, and her father shook his head.

"You have no energy either, lamb," he whispered. "And it is already nearly the end of November. At this rate, perhaps we should call off the wedding until we know what is wrong. You won't possibly enjoy your special day in the state you're in."

Dr. Neumann echoed her father's words later that day when her mother ushered her into his consulting room. "I'm going to have to send you to a specialist," he added grimly, scribbling something in his notepad. He tore off the top paper and handed it to Abigail.

"I recommend you go to Dr. Stanley Graham, at the county hospital, as soon as possible. I can no longer help you, I'm afraid, but he knows everything there is to know about the gastric system. Edith will be in excellent hands, I assure you."

Edith felt her heart drop into her shoes. Whenever the doctors sent people to the Englisch hospital, it didn't bode well at all. *Let's hope it's just a bump in the road,* she thought as she gazed into her mother's worried eyes.

Chapter 3
Diagnosis

On Christmas Eve morning, Edith struggled from her bed and trudged to the window. The fields were covered with pure white snow that also clung to the gnarled, reaching branches of the old maple tree that stood beside the house. Its twisted, bare boughs seemed to claw at the heavens, crying out for an answer to unuttered questions.

The sound of Silas's knock turned her attention away from the monochrome scene before her, but she didn't rush downstairs to be the first one at the door as she always had in days past. Instead, she struggled laboriously into her robe, shoved her feet into her sheepskin slippers, and made her way downstairs.

She could hear Hess answering the door and Silas's forced cheerfulness as he greeted her, asking if Edith was awake.

"I'm here, Sy," Edith answered before Hess could say she would look. She smiled weakly at him. The look on his face always pained her these days. She wanted him to look at her with that old look of adoring enchantment that he used to have. Now he just always looked worried. Except today, there was something else in his expression. Something undefinable to Edith. Or maybe she was just too exhausted to try to decipher it.

"Edie," he said, his voice quivering slightly. "I was at the post office to pick up our mail and I checked to see if there was any mail for your family, too." He paused, giving her a peck on the cheek.

"Jah? And?" Edith prompted, sinking down onto the sofa. Silas gingerly sat down beside her, as if he was afraid she would break if he accidentally bumped too hard against her.

"There's a letter for you from the county hospital."

His words were heavy with import. The Englisch doctor had said he would send a letter as soon as the results of her tests had come back. Through her pain and fatigue, her mind sharpened, and she looked into his eyes, exchanging a silent communication. *This is it. Now we know what the forecast is for our future.*

"Won't you read it, Sy," Edith breathed, leaning on his shoulder. "I don't think I have the gumption."

Silently, Silas tore open the envelope, extracted the crisp, neatly typed pages, and cleared his throat. "Dear Ms. Lapp. I have attached a complete workup of the test results with explanations below. We have also included a letter from Dr. Stanley Graham in which he suggests treatment suitable for your condition. Please contact our offices for information ... "

Silas paused, shuffling the papers. "Never mind all that, I'll read the doctor's letter first," he said, and then began reading again.

"Dear Ms. Lapp. I am so sorry to have to inform you of this, but at least the good news is that we know what is wrong and can recommend treatment going forward. Our tests have detected that you have a stomach tumor, and this is the cause of your great discomfort and pain. I recommend we begin a course of radiation treatment as soon as possible in order to shrink the tumor before we attempt to operate. After that you will need to undergo chemotherapy to ensure …"

"Please stop, Sy," Edith interrupted him in mid-sentence. It was already too much for her to deal with, without hearing the rest of the letter. Her mind grappled with the shocking diagnosis. A stomach tumor? *How, Gott? Why? Why did this have to happen to me?* The thoughts came without premeditation and she pushed them away.

"I'm so sorry, Edie," Sy said softly as a little sob reached Edith's ears. She looked up to see Hess sitting opposite them, tears streaming down her eighteen-year-old face.

"Are you going to die, Edie?" she asked in a quivering voice.

"I don't think so," Edith replied hesitantly, looking up into Silas's face.

"Doctor Graham seems to believe there is hope if you get treatment as soon as possible," he answered the question in her eyes, his own skimming through the rest of the doctor's letter. "It will be a long road to recovery and you might lose a bit of your stomach, but you should be able to live a fairly normal life. It depends if they can remove all the cancer, and it doesn't spread to other organs."

"I have some money saved from last summer," Caleb's voice piped up from the dining area. "You can have it for your treatment, Edie."

Edith sat up and twisted round to look at her little brother. He was barely sixteen and his voice had just broken, but already she could tell he was becoming a man. "But you've been saving so long for that German Shepherd pup you want," she began, but Caleb raised his hand, motioning her to silence.

"I'd rather have you around than a puppy," he said, his voice husky.

"Thank you, Caleb," Silas responded in an equally husky tone. "We can use that to start the community fund to pay for the hospital fees. I also have some savings I can put towards that."

Caleb nodded and rubbed his eye, pretending there was something caught under his eyelid, but Edith knew her little brother was secretly crying. She would have been a mess of tears herself if she were not so deathly tired.

"I'll go down to the Hochstetters' place and use their call phone," Silas announced, taking charge of the situation. "When we know how much all this will cost, we can get a community fund going. From what I can see in this letter, the sooner we get you into treatment, the better your chances of beating this thing."

Edith merely nodded and gave him a weak smile as he carefully embraced her and stood to his feet. The doctor had been right. There was some sense of relief in at least knowing what was wrong and being able to treat it. She would rather not think about the rigors of radiation treatment and chemotherapy. They had been all too clear to her when she had watched her Aunt Orpah wasting away from colon cancer.

Hess came to sit by her side as Silas let himself out of the house, intent on his self-appointed errand.

"Oh, Edie, this is just horrible. Now, who knows how long it will be before you and Silas will be married? I wish it were me instead of you."

Edith stroked her sister's hand. "I love you for saying so, Hessie," she said, meaning every word, "but you really must not even think such things. Everything is as Gott has ordained it to be."

"But why would He give you cancer? Right before your wedding? How could He do such a thing?" Hess sobbed, her lashes spilling over with fresh tears.

"Give me cancer? Why, Hess, God doesn't make us sick, He merely allows things to happen to us. This is nothing more than a trial. How can I only take what is good from Gott and reject Him when He allows things to happen that I think are bad?"

Hess stared at her sister, dumbfounded.

"Something good will come out of all this, my dear Hess," Edith continued gently. "I am being tested, as Job was, that is all. And I count it all joy, just as Paul told us to, that I am beset by this trial and testing."

Hess shook her head and stared at her hands. "I hope one day my heart will be as good as yours, Edie. Right now I am angry at Gott, if you must know."

"Please don't be," Edith pleaded softly, taking her sister's tear moistened hand and pressing it to her cheek. "I have you and Caleb and Maem and Daed. And I have Silas. What more blessings do I need, as long as I have you all to love and care for me?"

"Oh, Edie!" Hess buried her face in her sister's shoulder and wept.

"Promise me one thing, Hess," Edith added.

Hess nodded, her face still hidden.

"Promise me that tomorrow, on Christmas, we'll still celebrate the coming of Jesus Christ, the Savior, into the world. I want to focus on Him, the true Healer, and not on my illness."

Hess looked up into Edith's eyes. "I'll do anything you ask," she declared as the two sisters tenderly embraced.

Chapter 4
Fear and Faith

Nothing could have prepared Edith for the months that followed. The radiation therapy lasted only a few days, but the effects were much longer lasting, compounding her nausea, weakness, and pain. The doctor had used a combination of chemotherapy and radiation and it was wreaking havoc on her already emaciated body.

"You're young and strong, though I know you probably don't feel that way right now," he had explained gently at her first appointment for therapy. He had been right. She didn't feel young and strong, and the treatment had made her feel even less so.

Looking back, those weeks and months were an obscure haze of mental confusion, emotional upheaval, and physical agony that held few clear memories except for the stalwart presence and support of the people she loved most in all the world.

Everyone in the household had gone to enormous lengths to make things easier for her. They ate only what the cancer treatment team said she could eat. They kept their activities quiet and toned down so that she wouldn't become fatigued, but could still join in family times together. Her favorite thing was when Silas took her out on buggy rides.

He had fashioned a padded hammock in his buggy into which he would tenderly lift her and they would go for long rides around the countryside and talk and pray. The hammock meant that her fragile frame did not have to endure the bouncing and jarring of the buggy, which compounded her nausea and made every bone in her body ache.

It was on one such journey in the fall, a couple of days after the doctors had completed Edith's final round of chemoradiation therapy following her operation, that Silas drove her to a beautiful lake in the next county. He had brought along soft cushions and some of her favorite snacks—the ones that she could still eat—for them to share while they lay in the shade of the willow trees and threw cubes of bread to the ducks that paddled about on the serene blue waters.

Quietly, they spoke of their plans and hopes and dreams again, viewed in the light of the unexpected turn of events nearly a year ago that had changed everything in the twinkling of an eye.

"You know I thank Gott for you every day, don't you, Sy?" Edith asked him, reclining on the soft bed of cushions and basking in the peace that surrounded her.

"Well, that's good," he said with mock pragmatism. "Since I thank Gott every day for you, too, and we don't want things to get off balance here, do we?"

Edith laughed and then quickly grew sober again. "There isn't much left of me to be thankful for," she whispered. "Not after the chemo. My hair is all gone, and I make the bleached bones plastic skeleton in Miss Troyer's schoolroom look fat. There are very few men who would give me a second glance, let alone entertain thoughts of marrying me."

Silas leaned over and kissed her forehead. "That's because they don't know the Edie inside that skeleton," he said, and winked at her. Edith blushed.

Silas threw a handful of bread cubes at a duck that was venturing closer. "If I didn't stick with you, Edie, I wouldn't be deserving of you anyway," he said, with far more gravity. "This illness will pass. The person you are inside will never change. She will always be the precious Edie I've known all my life."

"Will she?" Edith queried thoughtfully. "I feel different from I did before. I feel like I've changed. Some things that mattered before, don't matter anymore."

Silas nodded slowly, holding her gaze. "That's true," he agreed. "I can't say that this journey has left me unchanged, either. But I'm thinking that perhaps it has made me a better person. I think I honestly didn't appreciate you as much before you got sick as I do now."

"I hate to admit it, but the same goes for me." Edie reached out and squeezed Silas's hand. "But I worry that this might not be the end. I've heard stomach cancer can be quite tricky to get rid of completely. What if it comes back? What if I'll never be my old self again? I mean physically, you know? What if I'm to be an invalid for the rest of my life?"

"Then Gott will help us deal with that. He'll never give us more than we can handle, you know that. Isn't it you who told me that is what gelassenheit is all about? When we know we can rest in Gott's faithfulness, we will not reach for anything else to give us security. We will be content in whatever situation we find ourselves in."

"I said that?" Edith felt surprised.

"You did," Silas affirmed.

"I think it must be the foggy brain syndrome Dr. Graham warned me about," Edith said with a shake of her head. "I swear sometimes I forget whether I'm coming or going. It's like my brain just checks out for a while."

"That too shall pass," Silas stated with affected pomp.

Edith laughed and threw a piece of bread at him.

"What!" he exclaimed. "Do I look like a duck to you?"

"No," Edith shot back with a mischievous grin. "But you are being a bit of a goose right now."

Silas gave an exaggerated gasp and feigned a tickle attack on her ribs. Edith laughed from the depths of her belly, knowing that if she had been in better health, they would have been rolling around on the grass at that point. It was a bittersweet observation that she kept to herself.

"If I never believed that a merry heart doeth good like a medicine, you have well and truly convinced me, Sy," she said once their laughter had died down again.

"May it be so," he replied tenderly, checking that the cushions were all still supporting her properly.

And then he suddenly prayed, staring out at the rippling waters of the lake with the afternoon sunshine flashing off the crests of each little wave and the ducks dipping down into its blue depths. The wind gently stirred his hair as if the hand of God himself were tousling his son's unruly mop.

"Dear Gott, danke that You have brought us this far. Danke that we know You are already in tomorrow and we can trust that You have already supplied us with all we need to bear whatever lies ahead for us. The doctors have done what they can and so have we. We know that healing comes from You alone and we pray for healing for Edie, Gott. Amen."

It was a few months later, on the first day of December, that Edith sat in Dr. Graham's consulting room, waiting for him to enter with the results of her latest tests. Silas's prayer had been so deeply etched on her mind that, despite everything else she forgot, she had repeated his prayer in her mind every single day since that sunny afternoon by the lake. She repeated it now again, word for word, her lips moving silently as her heart cried out to her Creator.

It wasn't lost on her that a year ago she had celebrated Christmas knowing that she could have been married already, living as Silas's wife, looking forward to the precious children they would bring into the world and raise to love God and people. Now all she wanted was to be cancer free.

As much as she loved her family and Silas for rallying around her and carrying her through the most difficult time of her life, she didn't want to be the invalid anymore. As much as she knew they had all carried the burden of her illness with love, she wished for their sacrifices to be rewarded.

For Caleb to get his German Shepherd pup; for Hess to have more time with her friends; for her to help her maem and daed around the house. Most of all, for Silas to have the wife he had waited so patiently for, for so many years.

She jumped at the sound of the door opening and Dr. Graham's voice giving a parting instruction to a nurse. Her heart thudded against her ribs as he walked around behind his desk and sat down. He had a large yellow envelope in his hand and pulled a printed sheet from it. His face was inscrutable, simply because he was the doctor who always seemed to smile, no matter whether he had good news or bad news to share.

He was smiling now as he looked at her over his half-moon glasses, his clear blue eyes comforting and fatherly.

Oh, dear Gott, let it be good news, please. The unvoiced prayer filled her and spilled out of her heart into the silent room.

Chapter 5
Hope Deferred

"Well Edie," Dr. Graham said, his characteristic smile still giving nothing away. "We have gone through all your tests with a fine-tooth comb, and I feel confident that we have a reliable result."

He paused. The air in the room seemed to pulsate with a life of its own as Edie hung on his lips, willing him to say the words she had been longing to hear for many months.

"You, young lady, are officially in remission."

Edith stared at him. Her mind grappling with the truth that Gott had answered her prayers, when she had been so given over to accepting whatever news she might receive.

"Remission," she repeated breathlessly.

"That's right." Dr. Graham's smile was a tad broader than usual, his eyes twinkling with satisfaction in a job well done. "Of course, you will need to come in for regular check-ups every six months, just as a precaution, but thankfully we caught the cancer early, before it could spread to other organs."

Edith felt giddy. *Danke, Gott, danke, danke, danke!* The prayer echoed in her mind as her eyes filled with tears of gratitude. She hardly heard anything more the doctor was saying. All she could think of was Silas and the wonderful, indescribable joy that filled her at the thought that their wedding dreams could still come true. There was still a solid three weeks before Christmas, more than enough time to prepare for a Christmas wedding.

"Doctor Graham," she blurted out during a brief pause in the good doctor's monologue. "I have to know, please. Does this mean that I am free to have my wedding? I think I told you we had to postpone because of the cancer?"

The doctor nodded, his smile still firmly in place. "Yes, you told me that. A few times," he said gently. "And, technically, you are free to have your wedding."

Edith sighed inwardly. Somehow, she knew there was a 'but' coming.

"But, in view of your weakened state, in my professional opinion, it would be better for you to hold off for a few months until you're stronger. Weddings involve some stress and the excitement itself can also take its toll on the body, more than we realize. Also, you won't enjoy your honeymoon half as much as you could if you wait until you're stronger."

Edith tried not to feel too disappointed. Dr. Graham's reply was an entirely reasonable one—a wise one, in fact, although she decided against correcting his assumption that Amish newlyweds had the kind of honeymoon that Englischers were accustomed to. Living with the bride's family while the couple built a new home was not exactly a holiday in Hawaii, as she had heard the Englisch dream honeymoon was.

She nodded submissively, considering the implications of what the doctor had said. A few months waiting would mean no Christmas wedding. *Hope deferred makes the heart sick …* the scripture verse crept into her mind. She steeled herself. Whatever happened, she could not allow her happiness to hinge on one hope.

"Thank you, Doctor Graham," she said, lifting her chin and smiling courageously. "I truly appreciate your concern and care for my welfare, and I will follow your wise advice."

"I had a feeling you would say that," Dr. Graham replied. "If you have questions or anything arises that causes you to worry about your health, don't feel like it is too small a thing to contact me and ask me about. If I am not available, someone on your cancer care team will be happy to help or refer your question or concern to me when I am reachable again." He rose from his seat and extended his hand.

"Thank you, Doctor," Edith replied, following his cue and rising from her own chair to shake the offered hand.

Later, as she sat ensconced in blankets beside a gently roaring gas heater, she told Silas all about Dr. Graham's good news—and not so good news.

"I have to agree with the doctor on this one, Edie," Silas said, apparently trying unsuccessfully to keep the disappointment out of his own voice. "It will be better for you to get back to your old energy levels before we have any kind of celebration, like a wedding. I know you. You'll say you'll take it easy, with the best of intentions, and then end up being the life and soul of the party."

Edith laughed softly. Nobody knew her like Silas did. It was one of the many reasons she loved him so much.

"You're right," she admitted in a melancholy voice. "We'll just have to let go of our dream of having a Christmas wedding. I don't think I'll have the self-control to bypass eating all my favorite sweet things like wedding nothings, anyway."

Silas placed his arm around her and drew her closer to him, where they sat on their favorite sofa. "Maybe not," he said, a brief glimmer of hope coloring his words.

Edith glanced up at him curiously. "What do you mean, Sy?"

"I mean, we've waited all our lives already. What's one more year? It's not like either of us is going anywhere, right? The elders are always talking about how the world is in a big hurry, but those who wait on Gott will be content to move with His times and seasons. And you're the one who told me that if we both have that desire, it must be Gott who put it there for a reason."

Edith snuggled up against her fiancé's warm bulk. "I need to be more careful about what I say to you," she said. "You remember my words far too well."

Silas's laughter rumbled in his chest and reverberated through Edith's body. "I hope you won't be too careful. The things you say have often challenged me to be a better man and helped me to see things from a broader perspective. I don't want to lose that, you know?"

Edith felt the warm thrill of affirmation run through her. Her only response was to snuggle even closer to the man she knew she could never deserve.

"Alright so we'll wait until next year Christmas before we tie the knot?"

"Jah, I think that will be the best. No stress, no hurry, more health and joy and peace. Works for me."

"Then it works for me, too."

They sat silently after that, just enjoying each other's closeness. No more words were needed, just the knowledge that the other was there. Edith felt a slow release as the sadness and disappointment faded away from her thoughts. Silas was right, as usual. There was no rush. They knew what they had in each other and they knew what they had in God. Times and seasons and marital status were of little consequence in the eternal scheme of things.

Edith let herself float along on the new sense of contentment that enfolded her. She closed her eyes, drawing in Silas's warmth and his faintly earthy, herby scent, absorbed from working by his father's side in the vegetable fields. She thought about the Englisch doctor and the patients she had seen in the hospital and wondered how many young women, or women of any age, had a man such as Silas in their lives.

His patience; his solid dependability; his quirky, slightly goofy wit; his unwavering faith. She felt nothing but compassionate pity for any woman who did not have what she had. *I am grateful, Gott,* were the last words that drifted through her mind before she sank into a deep, velvet sleep, her heart full and fully surrendered.

To some it might seem as if her hope had been deferred, but she knew, deep down, that her dream had already been realized; she already had all that she desired. She also knew that if she focused on that truth, it would be a tree of life and healing, not only to her, but to all those around her.

Chapter 6
Harvest Time

The cherry, maple, and sawtooth oak trees were just changing into their fall cloaks of vermillion, amber and burnt orange. The rows of pumpkins in the lower field were dying off, leaving the plump, segmented fruits of yellow and orange contrasted starkly against the dark, reddish earth. Edith stood on the porch and breathed in the cool crispness of the fall breeze tugging at the strings of her kapp. It felt good to be healthy again.

"Gut mariye, shaye maedel," a familiar deep, male voice broke in on her thoughts. She had forgotten what it felt like to feel beautiful, but Silas's words reminded her with crystal clear clarity.

She blushed as she turned her head to watch him climbing the porch steps and her heart skipped like a child in her chest. He was inspecting the little wisps of mahogany brown curls of hair regrowth that she just could not keep from peeping out from under her kapp, and his eyes held a look of utter enchantment. It was the look she had missed so much during the long months of her nightmarish illness.

He came to stand beside her, and she tilted her face for him to kiss her on the cheek. "Gut mariye, Sy," she replied.

"You're looking the picture of health," he said, beaming at her.

"I'm feeling it, too," she affirmed. "I had almost forgotten what it felt like to have energy, let alone being pain free or having an appetite. Do you know I had a second *and* third helping of Maem's cheese omelet this morning?"

Silas laughed. "I don't know of many brides who would boast about that a couple of months before their wedding." He winked at her.

"You know *plenty*, Silas Hauptfleisch," she retorted, "or have you forgotten that you're Amish?"

"Oh, I haven't forgotten, but I know a few of my fellow Amish who have conveniently adapted the meaning of beauty to suit themselves." He laughed and then sobered up. "Not that it is my place to judge them. Frankly, I'd rather have a healthy wife who isn't too pudgy."

"And not too skinny, either," Edith teased him.

He looked haunted for a moment. "Ach, du lieve, I didn't mean it that way ..."

"I know," Edith reassured him. "Are you ready to go deliver invitations?"

"As ready as I've ever been," Silas confirmed, holding his arm for her to take as they turned to walk into the house. Inside, Abigail had just finished binding a few different parcels of invitations. She looked up as the two lovebirds walked into the living room.

"Ah, there you are, just in time, Sy," she said in a brisk tone. "These are the ones for hand delivery, and these are the ones to go to the post office for the folks further away.

Zook's Corner is going to be a beehive in a couple of months."

She handed the bundles of invitations to Silas and Edith, and stepped back, smoothing down her apron and clearly satisfied with her work.

"Don't take too long, now, you hear? I'll be putting pork chops in the oven and roasting some vegetables for supper, so be sure to hurry home quickly when you're done."

"Jah, Maem, we will," Edith assured her mother. She looked at Silas as they headed for the door. "I can't believe it's really happening," she whispered excitedly.

The response to the invitations was overwhelming. By the time the sixteenth of December rolled around, they had received positive responses from almost every single one. Abigail was having a hard time figuring out where to put everyone since she had sent more invitations than they had seats, to compensate for those who would excuse themselves from attending.

"They're as excited as we are," Hess declared to the family sitting around the dining table and puzzling over their unexpected dilemma. "Everyone wants to see the miracle bride who beat cancer and is finally marrying the love of her life." She pressed her hands against her chest and breathed a little sigh of romantic bliss.

"Ach, come now, Hess," Edith chided playfully. "You make it sound like I'm some kind of Englisch celebrity."

Laughter filled the room.

"Well, I think anyone can see that what happened in your life is a miracle. I'll never forget Dr. Graham's face when you went for your last checkup. He said he himself could hardly believe you have even had cancer, and he was the one who performed the operation," Silas reminded her, his voice warm with gratitude.

"You're like Lazarus," Hess picked up where she had left off. "People came to see the miracle of his resurrection from the dead, too."

"Ach, du lieve!" Edith exclaimed. "I wasn't dead, Hess, just sick!"

Another round of uproarious laughter followed until a loud rapping on the front door broke through the joyful sound.

"I'll bet it's Grossdawdi Nathan," Caleb declared, jumping up from his seat and rushing to the door.

He was right. Abigail's parents had arrived from Ohio and a joyous family reunion took place before they took their luggage upstairs. As if on cue, they had just settled in the living room when the sound of a horse and buggy pulling into the driveway alerted the attention of the happy gathering.

"Grossdawdi Gabriel!" Caleb shouted ecstatically, leaping from his seat to get the door before his father's parents even set foot on the porch.

It was a deeply blessed evening for Edith. She hardly had to speak a word. Her story was told for her to the eagerly listening grandparents. Her doting family, including Silas, remembered some details even better than she did, and none of them left out any small step of the journey they had walked together through her sickness and recovery.

In between, Abigail and Edith cooked and served supper and then stories of other happenings in the family were exchanged from both sides. After all the catching up was done, and all had thoroughly enjoyed a sumptuous meal, Grossdawdi Gabriel leaned back in his chair, crossing his arms across his chest.

He was a tall man—a trait Edith's father had inherited from him—with startling green eyes and a shock of rich auburn hair that was streaked with gray. His beard was the same rich hue, and he stroked it now with a sunburned, calloused hand that yet showed considerable strength and dexterity. He rested his gaze on Edith and Silas, who sat together on a small two-seater sofa.

"I am so proud of both of you," he said, his deep voice warm and full of emotion. "It is a blessed day for any man to see his kin marry a solid member of the church who is kind, hardworking, and an authentic example of gelassenheit. I am grateful to Gott for letting me live to see this day."

Edith blushed and glanced sidelong at Silas. "It is your kinskind herself who keeps me on the straight and narrow many times, Grossdawdi," he said, inclining his head respectfully. "She is a true example of the Proverbs thirty-one woman. I thank Gott every day that He gave her to me."

Grossdawdi Nathan let out a guffaw. "That is by far the best reply I have ever heard from a young Amish bridegroom!" he declared, his bushy salt-and-pepper beard quivering with suppressed laughter. "Since we all know it is the truth that our wives secretly keep us in line, even while we try to convince each other that we are in charge of the household."

"Hush, Nathan!" Grossmammi Hannah chided him. "You'll give away *all* our secrets at this rate."

"You see what I mean?" Grossdawdi Nathan asked the company giving them a conspiratorial wink and a shrug.

Laughter erupted all around once more, and Edith joined in heartily. There were no words that could hope to fully describe the feeling of release and overflowing joy that sprang up in her heart. All the dark clouds and heavy burdens of her illness and the chemotherapy, not to mention the postponement of her marriage to Silas, had fallen away, and it felt like it bathed her in sunlight after a terrible hurricane.

She could breathe easy again. In little more than a week, they would be married and she could begin her life as Mrs. Silas David Hauptfleisch.

Grossmammi Hannah, who was sitting beside her, leaned over and whispered, "You are quite positively glowing, mei liebchen."

Edith squeezed her grandmother's hand and gazed at her fondly, her eyes brimming with tears. At last, her life was perfect. She and Silas had sowed in tears and soon they would reap the harvest with rejoicing.

Chapter 7
Family Home

Silas held out his hand and helped his bride-to-be down from the driver's seat of his buggy—soon to be *their* buggy. There was a light dusting of snow on the ground, so Edith's usually bare feet were ensconced in sturdy, black leather boots that Silas had bought her as a gift for her last birthday.

"Can you believe it's only five days before we finally become a family?" he asked her, his eyes locked on her face. She had never looked more beautiful to him.

"Jah und nay," she replied thoughtfully, smiling softly.

"You'll have to explain that one to me," he said, shaking his head.

"Jah, because I knew Gott would make all things work out when the time was right, and nay, because it felt like everything else was against us."

Silas took her hand and led her toward the old farmhouse that he inherited from his parents as his wedding gift. As the only son, and as the last to marry—his four sisters had all moved to their husbands' homes—he had been left the task of building a dawdihaus, and the privilege of being able to raise his family in the same house he had grown up in.

With a sense of great awe and gratitude, he opened the door for Edith and let her walk ahead of him.

"Oh, Silas! It's just how I imagined it would be!" she exclaimed, clapping her hands with joy as she turned slowly around and around, getting a good look at everything.

"There's still a lot of work to be done," he reminded her, "but Maem and Daed have already moved most of their things into the new cottage. If there's anything you want different, we can change it. This is our home, now, and I want it to feel that way for you, too."

"Oh, I'm sure I'll add some of my own things here and there. The linen chest my parents gave me will need a place to stand, and there's the piano that Uncle Titus promised me. Do you think one day we'll host worship here? I would love that, you know? And Hess has made some lovely quilts for us to …"

Edith stopped short, laying her hands across her chest. "Oh! Our clock! On the mantelpiece! It looks like it's been sitting there for generations!"

Silas stepped closer and draped one arm across her shoulders. "I thought the same thing," he said, not caring that his voice was husky from the lump in his throat. Edith turned her head to look up at him.

"It was all worth it, wasn't it, Sy? All the months of waiting, all the hospital visits and the chemo and the horrible side effects. I would do it again in a heartbeat if it was the only way I could stand here with you today."

Silas nodded. He didn't trust his voice. Drawing Edith closer to him, he kissed her tenderly on her temple. "I would hate to put you through all that again, but jah, it was worth it," he whispered.

They stood in silence for a while, watching the mahogany clock tick away the seconds. "Time really has no hold on us, does it?" Edith asked rhetorically.

"No," Silas agreed.

They stood quietly for a little longer. There were so many emotions churning about in Silas's heart and mind. Even if he had felt a need to express them in words to his betrothed, he knew he would not find the words. Besides, she didn't need to be told. She often seemed to assign more accurate descriptions to his feelings that he himself could ever aspire to.

But now was not the time for standing about mulling over feelings. His bride had to look over the rest of her new home. Silas took Edith's hand. "Let me show you what we have in the rest of the rooms," he said. "We can see what we'd like to change and start making plans."

The rest of the afternoon whisked by in a blur of trying out new arrangements for furniture, discussing where additional items could be placed or stored, planning the vegetable garden for the springtime and basking knowing that the way to their future together was opening up as smoothly as they had hoped it would.

"Let's just go say hello to your parents before you take me back home," Edith suggested, and Silas had no trouble agreeing.

Moments later, they stepped onto the porch of the newly built cottage and Silas rapped on the door.

"Kumm inseit," Naomi Hauptfleisch's voice filtered through the door. Silas opened it and they stepped into a room full of boxes in different stages of being unpacked, with the speaker herself moving about among the haphazard arrangement of cartons.

"Do you need help, Maem?" Edith asked, her eyes wide. It touched Silas's heart that his mother and his bride-to-be were already addressing each other as if they were blood kin.

"Ach, dochder, ney danke," came the gentle reply. "I hardly know myself what I want to do with all these things. I've been thinking it might be a good idea to send some of them back to the main house, if you're willing to take them back. Downsizing is proving not to be my strong point."

"She's not joking!"

Silas heard his father's voice ring out from the bedroom. He appeared in the doorway, his hands on his hips, but a broad grin on his face.

"I shudder to think what the Englischers' houses must look like if we, who are supposed to be Plain people, have so many things."

Silas laughed. "I almost feel bad for putting you in this position, Maem."

"Did you notice our son said he *almost* feels bad, schatz?" Benjamin Hauptfleisch queried with a ripple of laughter in his voice.

"I can't say I blame him. The reason he's kicking us out is that he's marrying the love of his life. Perhaps you've forgotten what that feels like." Naomi's voice held a tremor of humor that matched her husband's.

"Don't you believe that for a moment," Benjamin crossed the room and drew his wife closer in a warm embrace.

Naomi lay back in her husband's arms and Silas wondered if Edith looked quite as contented as that when she lay back in his arms. "Who's kicking you out?" he added, pretending to be hurt. "It was you who insisted that I take the main house and build the dawdihaus."

The only reply needed was Benjamin Hauptfleisch's loud guffaw. It was even more proof that his soon-to-be wife was already accepted into their family. Loud laughter was not something his father indulged in public. It was a side of him reserved only for the closest of family and friends.

"If you're sure there's nothing I can do to help, I'd best be getting back home," Edith said. "There is a lot to be done still before the twenty-fourth."

"Naturlich!" Naomi agreed amicably. "Off you go and we'll see you in a couple of days."

Silas and Edith took their leave and walked back to the stables to hook up Silas's gelding, Stef, to the buggy once more. As she helped to strap the bay horse into the traces, Edith paused and put her hand on Silas's arm. He stopped what he was doing, sensing that she had something important to share.

"You say you would not want to put me through that illness again, Sy," she whispered. "And you say it as if you did not suffer at all during that time, as if you didn't make any sacrifices or surrender any dreams, but I know you did. I saw it in your eyes. The worry, the fear, the determination, most of all, the deepest care. I don't think there are many who would do that."

Silas felt his throat constrict. She knew. Just as he had expected, she would. More than that, she had given the simplest and most sagacious of words to things he could not express.

"I haven't thanked you for sticking by me," Edith went on, seemingly aware that he was incapable of speech and comfortingly filling the silence. "I haven't thanked you for keeping the faith that our dream would come true, eventually. Thank you, Sy, thank you for never giving up on us."

Edith's eyes shone in the barn's dimness. Silas felt the jumble of emotions well up inside of him again, and all he could do was take her in his arms and hold her close to him.

"I love you, Sy. I love you so, so much," she whispered.

"I love you more, my little schnecken girl."

Chapter 8
The Blizzard

Two days after Silas had taken her to plan the arrangement of their new household, Edith sat writing and decorating place name cards at her parents' dining table. Hess had jumped in to help and Caleb was doing what he could to lend a hand, although the girls agreed he would make himself more useful by simply handing them the things they needed when they asked for them.

The front door opened and shut and soon Abigail appeared in the dining area, rubbing her hands together. "Ach, but the weather has turned suddenly foul," she remarked. "I was just at Betty's place, helping her with the preparations for the roasht when Gideon came in, telling us there's a blizzard on the way."

Caleb looked up sharply. "A blizzard? Will Daed be okay?"

"What do you mean, Cal?" Hess queried blithely. "Daed is in the barn, finishing the last of the wedding gifts."

"No, he's not. He had a call from that one Englisch client in Cabbage Hill, wanting his dining set earlier. He took it in the wagon with Horst and Hettie."

"He didn't tell me anything about that," Abigail countered, although the worry lines on her face had already deepened.

"I know, I was supposed to tell you, but I forgot," Caleb admitted sheepishly.

"Ach, Cal, I'll be so happy when this forgetfulness phase of yours has passed," Abigail ruffled his hair fondly. "When did he leave?"

"This afternoon just after lunch," Caleb informed the room unable to look his mother in the eye.

A moment of tense silence followed.

"He should have been back by now," Edith gave voice to everyone's thoughts. A stab of fear pierced her chest, but she forced herself to stay calm.

"If there is a team of horses that can get anyone home through a blizzard, it's Horst and Hettie," Abigail said, not sounding entirely convinced.

Edith looked up at her mother. "Let's pray," she said solemnly, but with a hopeful smile. "Gott tells us in His word not to put our trust in chariots and horses, but in the name of Gott."

"That is true, mei dochder," Abigail agreed, taking a seat beside her eldest daughter. The family, minus their father figure, gripped hands and prayed. Each one took a turn, pleading for the safety of Aaron and the two horses, as well as ministering angels, to guide them back home.

As the final chorus of amens rose around the table, there was a knock at the door. Edith's head shot up.

"Silas," she announced, immediately recognizing his familiar knock.

She ran to the door and let her shivering fiancé into the warmth of the heated interior. After a quick greeting, Silas looked around the little group.

"I went to the barn to help Aaron with the wedding gifts, but he's not there. I worked alone for a little while, thinking he'd be back soon, but it's been more than an hour now, and this snowstorm is getting really heavy. Do you know where he is?"

Edith shook her head. "The only thing we know is that he went to deliver a dining set to a customer, and he hasn't yet returned."

"Where?" Silas asked before Edith's words had time to grow cold.

"The customer lives on the other side of Lancaster, in Cabbage Hill," Caleb piped up, apparently feeling he was responsible for providing all the information that he could, since he had failed to do so in the beginning. "Daed said he lives on Purples Lane, the same man who ordered the walnut dresser a couple of months ago."

Silas nodded. "I know the place. I went with Aaron to deliver the dresser. They've bought a few things from us before. I'm going to look for him."

Edith felt the stab of fear again, this time like a sword twisting in her gut. "No, please, Silas, there's a blizzard coming!" she cried out, clutching his arm. After all the delays on their wedding day, and now being so tantalizingly close to their dreams being realized, she couldn't possibly allow him to go out in such dangerous conditions.

Silas covered her hand with his comforting warm one and looked into her eyes. "I know why you're worried, mei liebchen," he mumbled. "Trust that Gott will protect me. Your Daed needs me now, and it would be very wrong of me not to do everything I can to help him. He would do nothing less for me if it was the other way around."

Edith nodded, swallowing the fear and putting on a brave face. She knew Silas was right.

"Let me heat some tea for a flask and get you a bottle of my super tonic, in case he needs some when you find him," Abigail said briskly, shaking out her apron as she bustled off to the kitchen.

"Can't we just wait a little while longer?" Edith asked tremulously, hoping that she could delay Silas's leaving. "For all we know, Daed might be almost home already."

"If he is, then I'll find him quickly and we'll both be back soon." Silas wasn't giving in, but his tone was gentle and understanding as he placed an arm around her and squeezed her shoulders.

It was clear his mind was made up and nothing was going to change it. Edith knew she should be grateful—and she was—but she wished he could be brave and devoted to her family without putting his own life in jeopardy.

Abigale appeared with a canvas bag bulging with the promised tonics and some more reviving ingredients besides, so it seemed. She handed it to Silas. "Hessie, go fetch the thick woolen blanket off the foot of my bed."

Her youngest daughter obeyed and soon Silas was kissing Edith goodbye and promising them all he would take the utmost care and seek shelter if the blizzard grew too strong. When he had left, Edith stared out of the living room window, watching his buggy disappear down the road, swallowed up by the already howling wind and driven snow falling like a thick, white curtain.

She felt her mother's presence beside her before Abigail's fingers closed around her hand. "Just like we prayed for Daed, we can pray for him," she whispered. Edith nodded silently, the lump in her throat keeping her from answering. She knew it was wrong to fear, because fear showed a lack of faith in Gott, but she could not shake the sense of foreboding that weighed heavily on her heart.

"It's so close to our wedding day, Maem," she whispered hoarsely. "And we've waited so long already."

"Do you believe Gott is in your wedding, mei dochder?"

Edith turned her tear-streaked face to her mother's. She set her mouth in a firm line and nodded, feeling her heart flood with faith that was not her own, but could only come from One far more powerful that she was. "I do," she announced stoically.

"Then let's pray."

Chapter 9
His Return

The thick, swirling curtain of snowfall seemed to surround Silas in a bubble of isolation. He could see and hear nothing beyond a few feet all around him. The only sound was the howling wind and the creaking and squeaking of his buggy. Even his sturdy gelding's, hoof beats were muffled by the thick snow.

Not that they were moving fast enough for the horse's hooves to make any kind of loud sound. He knew that Aaron might have been stranded along the roadside at any point during his return and he didn't want to miss any telltale signs, like an overturned wagon lying on the shoulder of the road, so he kept the pace slow.

Besides, he could not afford to miss the turnoffs along the route, even though he knew it so well. Everything looked different from usual when it was blanketed in a white cloak of sameness. More than once, he wondered if he had missed a turn, only to come upon it later when he was about to turn back and retrace his steps.

The road was all but deserted. Now and then an Englisch car or truck with chains on the tires would crawl by him, going only slightly faster than he was. Silas hoped they could see his lantern burning from far enough away to avoid him if necessary.

As the time limped by and there was no sign of Aaron, Silas worried. He longed to wed his patient bride, but there was little chance they would have a wedding if Aaron was not found—or worse, found too late—by the time the wedding day rolled around. Another setback. Every year, another setback; another postponement.

Dear Gott, he prayed silently. *How many more times do we need to postpone? What is it that is not in place that we need to learn or discover? What have we done to deserve these constant trials?*

Even as he questioned his Creator, he felt a niggling sense of guilt in his gut. Besides the fact that it was selfish to worry about his wedding being postponed when his soon to be father-in-law could be fighting for his life somewhere in the icy, inhospitable elements, he knew Edith would not let him entertain such rebellion as he was in those moments.

Throughout their difficult years of struggling against cancer, waiting for Edith's health to improve after she had gone into remission and now finally standing on the brink of the realization of their dreams, she had not once wavered in her faith.

Gott does not owe us anything, Sy. Her words echoed in his mind while his eyes scanned the roadside for any signs of an upturned wagon or a stranded pair of Percherons. *How can we praise Him only when he gives us good things in life? He is all knowing and we are not. That knowledge should be sufficient for us to trust that He knows what is good for us, even when it feels awful.*

"Dear Edie," he whispered to himself. "You're a much better person than I am. I almost think I do not deserve to marry you. Perhaps that is why we are not married yet. I have not yet learned to trust as you have."

He was so deep in thought as he continued to scan the roadside that he did not notice how fast he was going. Nor did he notice the buggy was cresting a rise. Before he knew it, Bernard was digging into a thick sheet of glassy ice with his carbide spiked winter shoes, but the momentum of the buggy was too much for any horse to handle.

Despite the gelding's most valiant attempts, the buggy skidded sideways and careened down the hill. Silas stepped on the brakes, but he hit them too hard and only helped to make the skid worse. Bernard, clearly confused at the sensation of being dragged backwards down a hill by the contraption that usually followed along behind him, bucked and kick, desperate to free himself.

Silas was helpless to do anything but grip the edge of the driver's seat and try to keep his balance. The frantic horse kicked himself free and went galloping off into the snow. The buggy, released from the weight of the horse, crashed over onto its side.

Silas felt himself falling, felt the jarring thud of rock-solid sheet ice against his shoulder and his skull sending needles of pain through his whole body. Then everything went black, and he felt himself slipping away. Whether it was the rest of the way down the hill, or only into unconsciousness, he could not tell.

***

Edith sat by the window, her place name cards done and decorated, with nothing to occupy her mind except her missing father and Silas, who was out there in the howling blizzard, looking for him. *Was it foolish of us to let him go?* she asked God silently in her heart. *How much can one really see in the middle of a snowstorm? Should we have waited until the storm let up? But then what if Daed is really in trouble and would have frozen if we waited too long?*

"Don't torture yourself with too many questions, mei liebchen," her mother's voice sounded unexpectedly beside her.

Edith jumped with fright and looked up into her mother's gentle face. "How did you know what I was thinking, Maem?"

"I've known you since you drew your first breath. How could I not know what's going on in your mind?" her mother replied with a counter question and a soft smile. "I know that look on your face all too well."

Edith smiled wanly in return and leaned against her mother's comforting bulk. "So many questions and not a single answer," she lamented sadly. "All I can do is wait here and hope I will see a wagon and a buggy pulling up the driveway before the darkness sets in tonight. And that's not all that far away."

She glanced at the clock. The hour hand was advancing relentlessly towards the number seven and the brilliant white of the swirling snow outside was already fading to a soft dove gray.

"Would you like me to sit here with you?" Abigail offered.

"Ach, Maem, how I wish I could be as selfless as you are. You must be worried sick about Daed, and yet you are the one who has words of comfort to offer, while I think only of my own heartache. I'm so sorry." Edith wrapped her arms around her mother's waist and hugged her. The older women lifted her arm over her daughter's head and returned the embrace.

The two women sat in silence, watching the light fading slowly from the snowy scene outside the window. Edith did not know how much time passed, but all at once, she realized the snow had lessened and the wind had stopped howling. Soft, white flakes fell gently to the ground like tiny feathers and she realized she could once again see beyond the fence and a little way down the road.

A movement caught her eye. She blinked, wanting to make sure she was not mistaken, and focused hard to see beyond the thinning curtain of frozen precipitation. Two black faces, with matching white blazes running from forelock to muzzle, appeared out of the formless whiteness, nodding and swaying as they pulled against the weight of the wagon behind them, lifting their hooves high out of the knee-deep snow.

"Maem! It's Horst and Hettie!" Edith cried, jumping up from her seat by the window. Abigail looked up, her eyes searching and hopeful.

"You're right, Edie! It is! Oh, danke Gott!" Her hands flew to her mouth as her eyes glistened with tears. The clattering of feet on the stairwell echoed in the room and soon Hess and Caleb were by their side, peering through the window.

The two black Percherons turned in at the driveway and headed straight for the barn, driven by a lone, hunched, blanket-shrouded form on the driver's seat. Abigail rushed to the door and flung it wide. Hess and Caleb followed behind her without missing a beat as she ran out onto the porch, down the steps and towards the barn.

Edith wanted to follow, but her feet seemed to be nailed to the floor. Her father was back, but where was Silas? Where was Bernard and the buggy? Why had her father returned alone? The old fear clutched stubbornly at her heart again as she willed her fiancé to appear on the road and turn into the driveway behind her father.

The empty road seemed to mock her as falling snowflakes slowly filled the wagon's tracks.

Chapter 10
The Foundling

Silas woke to throbbing pain coursing through his whole body. He could not feel his fingers or toes and his eyes seemed frozen shut. As his mind swam to the surface of consciousness, he heard voices whispering.

"This has to be the one," a deep, gravelly voice said.

"I think you're right," a warm, husky female voice replied.

"Help me here, schatz," the man's voice entreated.

Silas felt hands gripping his arms. He groaned.

"He's conscious," the woman noted. "You're safe, youngi. We've got you," she assured him, compassion filling her voice.

Silas groaned again, unable to form words. He allowed himself to be half dragged, half carried to a wagon of some sort, that seemed to be hitched to a tractor, if the sound of the engine was anything to go by. He pressed his hands against his face, but he could feel nothing. Everything was numb and useless.

The jostling of the wagon sent pain shooting through his entire body, but he gritted his teeth and tried not to moan too much. Whoever these people were, they were saving his life, and he instinctively didn't want them to think he was ungrateful.

Thankfully, it was not a long ride to their home and soon he found himself stripped of his frozen clothing, wrapped in a fluffy toweling robe that ostensibly belonged to the kindly gentleman, and seated in front of a roaring fire. The ice had quickly thawed off his eyelashes, and he could see again. With curiosity, he noticed the fire was behind glass and seemed not to be actual flames, yet gave off heat as fierce as any gas heater he had sat beside.

The couple who had so kindly rescued him turned out to be a fairly elderly pair of Pennsylvania German folk who were neither Amish nor Mennonite. The old lady insisted he drink an entire mug of hot ginger tea with far too much honey, assuring him that was intentional. He needed the sweetness for the shock, she said.

As he sat shivering in front of the strange fake fire, he felt the feeling slowly returning to his frozen limbs. His fingers and toes, and even his nose and cheeks, stung and tingled painfully, but he was grateful. He would have had bigger problems if his nerve endings had felt nothing. As a welcome distraction from the torturous pins and needles sensation, he listened to the kindly couple tell him of their history and why they were familiar with the Pennsylvania Dutch language.

"We left the Anabaptist church a long time ago," the old man told him without a hint of bitterness in his voice. "It was simply a call to a different way of worship," he explained, smiling warmly. "We lived in Harrisburg before we moved here and started our little cabbage farm."

Silas nodded, still feeling too dazed to offer an intelligent response.

"Where are you from, my dear?" the woman asked him. "We'd like to help you get back home, or at least let your folks know where you are."

Silas stared at her, wanting to answer her question but finding his mind a total blank. He didn't even know what his last name was, let alone where he came from.

"I ... I'm not sure," he stammered uncertainly. "I feel like I should know, but ..." His voice trailed off.

"Ach du liebe!" the woman exclaimed sympathetically. "Well, don't you worry about it at all, young Silas. We have your horse in our barn, and we've arranged for a neighbor to bring your buggy over. Just you thaw out and rest up. Perhaps when you've had some sleep, you'll remember."

Silas nodded obediently, a hollow feeling yawning in the pit of his stomach. He felt an inexplicable urgency to know where he came from. It was as if there was somewhere he needed to be, someone who was waiting for him, someone he could not afford to let down, but that was as far as his knowledge went.

As frustrating as that partial knowledge was, he knew Gertrude, as the kind old lady had introduced herself, was right. After their simple evening meal of bread, cheese, and pickles, they allowed him to make use of their bathroom and he readied himself for bed. The arms and legs of the old man's borrowed pajamas were a little short, but otherwise they fit comfortably.

When morning came, he sat up, staring around the room, at first feeling panicked and not knowing where he was. Then the events of the previous day came filtering back. He could remember being picked up from the frozen ground by the friendly folks whose guest bed he now lay in, but everything before that was a blur. Images of a horse kicking at the traces and a buggy sliding uncontrollably across a slick sheet of ice were all that came to him.

His head ached, and he felt slightly nauseous, but the urgency to know who he was had returned in full force. Keeping his movements as smooth as he could for fear of jarring his already pounding brain, he washed up and dressed in the clothing provided. Again, the arms and legs were too short, but he didn't care. Making his careful way to the kitchen, he discovered it was already late morning and his benefactors had eaten breakfast hours before.

"Ah, there you are!" David, the old man, exclaimed as he entered the room. He appeared to be engaged in fixing some sort of electric appliance. "We thought we'd let you sleep as long as you needed to. Can't rush these kinds of things, you know? Would you like some breakfast? Gertie has it keeping warm for you."

"That's awfully kind of you, danke," Silas replied, wondering how he was going to keep down a plate of bacon and eggs, but not wanting to refuse David's kindness. "I think I'll have it when I come back, if you don't mind," he compromised, buying himself and his unhappy stomach some time. "I'd like to go look at my horse and buggy, if that's alright. I'm hoping the sight of them will jog some memory."

David widened his eyes. "What a gut idea!" he enthused. "Come, I will take you there. It's near to the house.

Silas gratefully accepted and followed his new friend outside to the barn. All the way, David entertained him with the story of how he and Gertrude had been quietly whiling away their evening building a jigsaw puzzle and knitting, respectively, when they heard the thunder of hooves and a large, bay horse with a harness but no buggy behind him came flying past their living room window.

When they reached the barn, David switched on the electric light and the brightness dazzled Silas for a moment. He blinked and then realized he was looking at a long equine face, with a large star shaped marking on the forehead, peering at him curiously. The horse gave a deep throated nicker and extended his muzzle toward Silas.

"I think his name is Bernard," he said cautiously, moving forward and scratching the horse behind his ears. Bernard whinnied softly and rubbed his head against Silas's shoulder.

"Well, will you look at that? The poor ol' feller's telling you he's sorry for smashing up your buggy," David remarked with a chuckle.

"May I see the buggy?" Silas asked, wondering if that was a good idea at all.

"Sure, it's over there," David responded, pointing past Silas's left shoulder. Silas turned and gasped. The horse-drawn vehicle was in a state of disrepair that even he, with his memory loss, knew would take more than a few hours to fix. His heart sank. He didn't know where he came from, and he didn't have any means of transport, and yet there was still that unshakable, nagging urgency that he had to be somewhere soon.

Suddenly, he gasped again. The memory of the accident flashed in crystal clarity before his mind's eye. "I was looking for someone," he said. "Someone who went missing. And then we went over the crest of the hill and hit that sheet of ice. I wasn't paying attention to the road because I was looking for a stranded wagon."

He turned to face David, who nodded encouragingly, as if urging him to continue.

Once more Silas' heart sank. That was all he could remember. He was looking for a missing person. And now he was a missing person himself. The irony was stupendous. But worse than that, his remembering had only compounded his confusion. He knew the missing person he had been looking for was not the person who was waiting for him to return to wherever he came from.

Feeling defeated, he turned and left the barn, his shoulders slumped and his head aching worse than ever.

"Don't worry, youngi," David commiserated, following close on his heels. "You'll figure it out soon enough. Every bit you remember is progress."

Silas nodded and smiled at him gratefully. He didn't want to tell the kindly old gentleman that he worried his remembering might come too late.

Chapter 11
Hope is All Things

The blizzard that had started everything was already a memory, but it's devastating effects were still operating in full force. Edith stood by the window staring almost sightlessly out at the empty road, her sight blurred by unshed tears that she stubbornly kept blinking back.

"Boppeli," her father was saying gently, "this is no time to be sad, although I understand your heartache. Your maem is right. It will be best to call off the wedding until we find Silas. There's nothing more we can do."

He was talking to her in the voice he had always used when she was a little girl, and she needed some gentle reprimand. She loved him for it. She had always believed her father was the kindest, gentlest father any girl in their community had. But she could not agree with his words.

Brushing the tears from her lashes, she turned from the window to face him and Abigail, who were watching her with concerned frowns furrowing their foreheads.

"Is there truly nothing more we can do?" she asked, trying not to sound challenging. She had never challenged her parents in anything before and it felt strange to do so now, but there was something stronger inside of her, something she could not ignore.

"You know that nearly all the young men in the village are out searching for our Silas," her mother reminded him. "Do you think we don't care for him, that we're just giving up?"

"Ach, Maem!" Edith exclaimed, feeling fresh tears springing to her eyes. "Of course I know you care for him! And of course I know you're not just giving up. But I can't cancel my wedding. I just can't. And I can't even explain to you why. I know that he's going to find his way back here. I just know it."

She lifted her hands and let them drop limply to her sides in exasperation. If only she could make them understand, but how could she, when even she didn't understand what was happening in her heart and mind and spirit?

"We're believing for that with you, mei dochder," her father assured her tenderly. "But maybe it will be better to let everyone go back home instead of keeping them here, waiting indefinitely."

Edith shook her head, unable to prevent the tears from spilling over onto her cheeks. "My wedding is tomorrow, Daed. Tomorrow. Just one more day. I am sure they can all wait one more day." Her tone was pleading, her voice unsteady.

Abigail stepped forward and took her daughter's hand. "We're worried that all this is too much stress on you, especially since your illness and …"

"Ach, Maem, I love you both for that, but I beg you, please, don't postpone the wedding, at least not until the 24th is over. We were all going to spend Christmas together, with or without a wedding."

"It was never about the family, boppli," her father croaked hoarsely, tears shining in his own eyes. "It was always about taking the pressure off of you."

Edith flung herself into her father's arms. "This is how you can do that," she said into his ear as he embraced her in his big bear hug she knew so well. "Don't call off the wedding, not until I say it's time. Please Daedi."

Abigail stood beside them, rubbing the small of Edith's back the way she used to when Edith was a little girl and couldn't fall asleep at night. She imagined her parents talking to each other with their eyes, as she had so often seen them doing.

"Alright, mei liebchen," Abigail agreed at last. "You call off the wedding when you think it's time. You're right, we're all here for Christmas, anyway."

Edith drew back and took her mother's hand once more. "Danke, Maem," she said with soulful sincerity.

"Well," Aaron said slowly, "if we are still preparing for a wedding tomorrow, I believe there are still many things to be done, right?"

"Jah, indeed there are, mei mann," Abigail agreed with great gravity. "No time for anyone to be standing staring out of windows."

Edith smiled through her tears and managed a shaky laugh. "I see what you two are doing," she told them. Her father's eyes went wide as saucers as he shrugged in feigned innocence, while her mother simply laughed.

"Come, liebchen," she said, drawing Edith toward the front door. "Those celery sticks will not jump into the vases by themselves."

Edith wiped her eyes with her dress sleeve and dutifully followed her mother to the coat rack, bundling up before stepping out onto the porch and hurrying to the barn where the tables had been set up. A crowd of family and friends were sitting and standing around, looking uncertain as mother and daughter stepped inside and closed the door behind them.

Abigail cleared her throat. "Mei lovely friends and family," she addressed them in her best teacher's voice. "We are still uncertain about our beloved bridegroom's whereabouts, but his faithful bride has decided she will not give up hope that his coming will be in time for the feast we have prepared."

A murmur of voices rose in the large interior as this piece of news was discussed. Abigail held up her hand, and the room fell to order once more. "We will go ahead as planned until the time when the wedding is to begin. When that time comes, we will respond according to whatever has developed in the interim. Danke so very much for holding our hands in this difficult situation. We love and appreciate you all deeply."

A burst of spontaneous applause broke out and Edith hugged Abigail. There really was no other woman she would have wanted for a mother. As stubborn as she could be sometimes, there were moments like these when it was clear her life was inseparably wrapped up in the lives of her children.

The gathered helpers resumed their tasks, seeming grateful to keep their hands busy, as if they also needed distraction from the nagging worry that the bridegroom might not arrive in time for the long awaited and oft postponed ceremony.

Edith and Abigail fell to trimming the stalks of celery that Aaron had ordered from the large fresh market in the Englisch area and arranging them in jars in the middle of each table. At one end of the barn, gas cookers had been set up and food was being prepared as far as was possible on the day before Edith and Silas' big day.

"You know, Maem," Edith said thoughtfully while she sliced off a few ragged and wilted leaves from a stalk she was trimming, "all of this reminds me in some ways of the way the Bible describes the church as the bride of Christ. We don't know when He is coming, and yet we wait patiently and keep alert, preparing ourselves for that day as if it were to come tomorrow."

Abigail paused in her work. "Ach, dochder," she replied, her voice cracking with emotion. "You always were one who could see the hand of Gott in everything, since you were but a little thing."

"Ach ney, Maem," Edith responded, her cheeks flushing. "I am no saint, but it brings me comfort to think of things in that way. I can't explain any of this. I only know I have to keep the faith. Silas would want me to."

She paused, lowering her eyes as a new thought struck her. "Perhaps all of this is Gott's way of teaching me something. Perhaps Silas and I have been so caught up in *our* day and *our* dream of a Christmas wedding that we've sort of forgotten Him. Perhaps this is just His way of reminding us that everything really is about Him."

Abigail took Edith's free hand and kissed it. "Gott bless you, mei kinder," she breathed. "Your heart is wholly His."

Edith hoped her mother was right. The test still lay ahead. It was not December 24th yet.

Beareth all things, believeth all things, hopeth all things, endureth all things, a sliver of scripture verse from her most beloved passage of the Bible, 1 Corinthians 13, describing the attributes of love, rose in her mind.

Jah, Gott, she prayed silently. *My love is being tested in so many ways I could never have imagined. I don't know if I can pass this test on my own. Please, please help me.*

Despite there being no answer, internal or external, to her plea, she felt an inexplicable peace settle upon her. In that moment, she knew whether Silas made it back in time for their wedding or not, her heart would be at peace. If she truly loved God above all else, including Silas, it could be no other way.

Chapter 12
The Floodlight

Silas couldn't remember ever sleeping as much as he did in the two days after his accident. During the few daylight hours that he could keep his eyes open, he tended Bernard's wounded legs, feeling thankful that the horse had not badly injured himself and gone completely lame.

David was a great help, too. Although he didn't have any horses of his own, just a milk cow and a small herd of sheep, he clearly missed having an equine on his farm. He still knew exactly what concoctions to throw together to speed up the healing in the gelding's legs.

"I had a horse once, did exactly what yours did, except he wasn't sliding down an ice-covered slope. The stubborn creature had decided he would not work on a Sunday and kicked himself loose while we were driving over to a neighboring farm for church. He was a youngster then, and feisty as well as being a big-boned horse. I wanted to use him for breeding, but that brief episode changed my mind. He was gelded within a week after that."

Silas laughed and Bernard nibbled at his hair while he applied some poultice to the horse's shins. It was glaringly obvious that the horse had only barely cleared some fences on his way onto David's property. Or perhaps not cleared them at all and David was too kind to mention it.

"Bernard wasn't gelded because of his temperament," he offered. "At least I don't think so. I bought him from a friend who left the community after his rumspringa. He's always been dependable. I'm sure the accident was my fault. I probably wasn't paying attention to the road."

"He sure looks pretty fond of you," David noted in agreement. "Makes me wish I could have just one around, but these old bones won't manage climbing up and down from a horse and we've no use for a buggy around here."

"I suppose a horse isn't necessary when you can use a car without being put under the Bann," Silas said, hoping David would not think him flippant.

"We don't have a car, either," David replied, not seeming to notice anything untoward in Silas' comment. "We've cycled to the little shopping mall down the road when we need supplies or an outing, but mostly we just get things delivered. That's one thing I enjoy about being an Englisch." He winked at Silas and smiled in a fatherly way.

Silas smiled back, considering how ironic it was that he could never think of David as an Englisch. He seemed just as Amish to Silas as his own father. As the thought crossed his mind, Silas caught his breath.

"I remember my father," he said, pausing in his ministrations to Bernard's shins.

"Was he the one you were looking for?" David inquired, his eyes bright with hope on Silas' behalf.

Silas shook his head, scowling in frustration as the flimsy memory seemed to disappear like a puff of smoke even as he grasped at it to hold it fast and keep it clear. "I don't think so, but I can't be sure. Strangely enough, I feel like the person I was searching for is someone equally important to me as my father. Can that be possible?"

David looked thoughtful. "I know Gertie's father was as much a father to me as my own. Even after we left the church, he still secretly made plans to visit us more than once. It was a miracle the bishop never found out. He's gone to a better place now, bless his soul."

Silas felt perplexed. He didn't feel like he was married, and yet he had a memory of a man who was as important as his father. "Perhaps he's more like a mentor. I can't imagine I'd remember my father-in-law before my wife."

"Jah," David agreed, slowly nodding his head. "That would be quite unusual." Then he brightened. "But there it is, another memory. No matter how small, it's a step in the right direction."

Silas appreciated his new friend's positivity and wished he could fully embrace it. In the back of his mind, a clock was ticking, but he couldn't read the dial and he didn't know why the alarm bell was about to go off.

The next morning, he woke and stared up at the ceiling above him. It was the same ceiling he knew he had slept under for the last three nights, but this morning, it somehow looked different and new. He rubbed the sleep out of his eyes and stretched. The sense of that day being an important one stirred in his mind. Still groggy with sleep, he sat up and looked around the room.

The predawn gray revealed his own clothes hung over a chair, with his boots scrubbed and polished beneath it. His hat hung on a hook on the door of his room and below it hung a calendar with a scene of rolling farmlands. His eye roved along the weeks and then he realized it was the week of Christmas.

Oh! Today must be Christmas, he thought to himself. He stood up from the bed and crossed over to the ensuite bathroom. Brushing his teeth and combing his hair just for the sake of being respectful towards his gracious hosts, he tiptoed into the living room. For the first time, he noticed the small Christmas tree and carved wooden nativity scene in the corner, wondering vaguely why he hadn't seen it before.

He didn't ponder on it long, though. He was simply grateful that his head was feeling clearer than it had since he had first limped into the farmhouse, supported by its two elderly inhabitants. He stepped through to the kitchen, the sound of teaspoons clinking against ceramic mugs drawing his attention.

"Merry Christmas!" he greeted as he entered.

David and Gertrude looked up from their mugs and stared at him. Then Gertrude seemed to realize.

"Ach du liebe, that bump on your head has set you all awry. It's the twenty-fourth today, schatz, Christmas is only tomorrow," she said kindly, not mockingly at all.

Silas stopped in his tracks. The twenty-fourth of December? Why did that feel like such an important date? Then clarity hit, as if someone had switched on the floodlight that the Englisch liked to use when they played sports at night.

"It's my wedding day today," he blurted out, feeling his heart pound frantically and his hands shake. He also felt thankful that he was not holding a mug of coffee in his hands. It would have been smashed at his feet on the flagstone floor.

If he thought he was shocked at his own discovery, David and Gertrude looked even more so.

"Your wedding day?" Gertrude echoed, clearly still processing his words.

"My wedding day!" Silas exclaimed, the full measure of all his memories flooding back at once. The mahogany clock on the Christmas he had asked Edith to be his wife; the terrible news of her illness the next year; the relief at finding out she was in remission the Christmas after that; the decision to wait one more year; the knowledge that finally their day was drawing near, only to have her father go missing in a blizzard days before their long-awaited dream was to come true.

Silas recounted the complete tale to his two wonderful rescuers, who sat and listened in silence, never once taking their eyes from his face while their coffee grew cold unheeded in their mugs on the kitchen table.

"And that's why I was out here on this side of Lancaster," Silas concluded. "I had to find Aaron and take him back home in time for the wedding."

"Wunderbar!" Gertrude cried out, clapping her hands together excitedly. "That your memory returned on this day of all days!"

Silas nodded, returning her ecstatic grin, and then he grew somber as he remembered something else.

"But I don't have a buggy, and you don't have a car," he gave voice to the sudden panic that rose in his throat. "How am I going to get back to Zook's Corner in time? It's hardly likely I'll find transport now. Everyone will be doing last-minute preparations. Nobody's going to …"

He didn't finish his sentence. David's hand rested on his arm, silencing his fearful babbling.

"Do you think Gott would give you your memory back on your wedding day if He didn't intend for you to make it back in time?" he asked, his eyes grave but compassionate.

Silas swallowed. "But how …?"

"I suppose there's only one way to find out," Gertrude said with a little smile in her voice. "Technology." She pulled a smartphone out of the pocket of her robe.

Silas' eyes grew wide. "I don't know if …" he began, but Gertrude cut him off with a wave of her hand.

"Of course you can't use it," she stated with a mischievous twinkle in her eye. "But we can."

Chapter 13
A Tree of Life

Edith didn't want to open her eyes. She already knew she would see one of two things: the empty road that had taunted her for the last three days without mercy, or Silas's beloved face at the front door, announcing that he was home, and ready to be united with her in marriage. The fear of the first possibility outweighed the second by far, no matter how valiantly she tried to steel herself against it.

She could hear the sounds of the first sleepy roosters crowing and the first hesitant chirps of the fledgling dawn chorus. There was also the sound of activity in the kitchen and she knew her mother would be up already, getting ready to put the final finishing touches to the feast that awaited their guests.

It would all be worthless if Silas wasn't there.

Was I foolish, Gott? To insist that we go ahead without knowing whether Sy would make it in time? The question drifted into the space of the surrounding room. There was no response, no whispering in her heart, no quiet, inexplicable knowing, just a gaping, aching emptiness. Then, without warning, a scripture verse dropped into that yawning abyss.

For we are saved by hope: but hope that is seen is not hope: for what a man seeth, why doth he yet hope for? But if we hope for that we see not, then do we with patience wait for it.

Edith squeezed her eyes shut tighter. *It's so hard, Gott, so hard!* She cried out from the depths of her spirit.

For a few moments longer, she lay there and then the sounds from the kitchen seemed to grow louder. *If nothing else, the least I can do is honor the fact that my parents honored my request not to call of the wedding and bring my part to be ready,* she thought to herself.

It was enough to get her out of bed and into her robe. She washed and dressed in one of her everyday dresses before braving the realm beyond her door. The kitchen was already a hive of activity. Both grossmammis were there, lending a hand as Abigail bustled about. Now and then someone would break out into song or stop and breathe a prayer for Silas's safe return. Each time, the others in the room would join in, or add a lusty, "Amen," in agreement.

Edith kissed her mother on the cheek in greeting and took over the mixing of the dough she was making so that Abigail could begin working on the sauce that was to go with it. Before she did, Abigail paused and gave her daughter a long, probing look.

"Are you sure you're still okay with going ahead, dochder?" she asked gently. Her eyes told Edith she was giving her a way out, a chance to go back on her decision, and at that same time assuring her that if she went on, Abigail would support her every step of the way. Edith's heart swelled with gratitude. She nodded.

"Jah, Maem," she whispered. "As Daed always likes to say, 'Difficulty is a miracle in its first stages.'"

Abigail gave her daughter a quick hug. "I am so proud of you, Edie," she said hoarsely and went off to collect the ingredients for the sauce.

As each stage of the preparation was completed and there was still no sign of Silas, Edith felt her faith failing. Like a woman hanging from a cliff ledge, her fingers slipped closer and closer to the edge of the only thing that was keeping her from plunging into an abyss of despair. Although everyone around her was trying to put on a brave face, the faintest shadow of pity had crept into their eyes. Edith focused on their smiles, rather than their eyes.

At last it came time for her to dress into her wedding dress. She knew Silas's wedding clothes were laid out in the guest room of their house and her heart ached. If only he could have been there already. He might have missed all the preparations, but at least she could don her cobalt blue wedding dress with a lighter heart than the one that now beat dully in her chest like a rusted water pump.

Abigail came into the room to find her sitting on her bed, wrapped in her robe, and staring at the dress hanging against the wall.

"It's time, Edie," she said, sitting down beside her daughter. "Let's get you dressed."

Edith leaned against her mother's shoulder without answering.

"Remember you told me about the bride of Christ who doesn't know when her bridegroom is coming?" Abigail asked softly, her voice barely above a whisper, yet it seemed like shouting to Edith's ears.

"Jah," the young bride replied, wishing she hadn't come up with that comparison.

"Do you think He would want us to give up preparing ourselves just because He took longer than we would like him to?" Abigail added to her questioning.

The lump in Edith's throat prevented her from answering, so she merely shook her head.

"How about we take a deep breath, do whatever we can from our side and leave the rest to Gott?" Abigail concluded.

Edith took a deep breath, releasing it in a long, drawn-out sigh. "That is fair," she agreed. "That *is* what I said I would do, and it's only right that I follow through."

"Brave girl," Abigail encouraged her. "If Silas could see you now, I know his heart would burst with happiness."

Steeling her resolve, Edith stood up and lifted the dress down from the wall.

The dressing process progressed in silence. Abigail pinned the cape and apron in place and then took the brand new white kapp from Edith's dresser. She placed it tenderly on her daughter's head and pinned a few wayward curls into submission. Then she stepped back and surveyed her handiwork.

"You are a pure bride," she declared, her voice filled with deep contentment.

Edith smiled wanly. "And now we wait for the bridegroom."

As mother and daughter walked arm in arm down the stairs to the front door of their family home and out across the yard shoveled and swept clear of snow by the male guests, Abigail shared one last bit of wisdom with her daughter.

"I'm reminded of the parable Jesus told of the ten virgins," she said. "Do you remember how they all fell asleep, but some kept their lamps trimmed and full of oil?"

"Jah, I do," Edith affirmed, wondering where her mother was going with the story.

"I've often thought that oil is the oil of joy spoken of in Psalm Forty-Five. I may be wrong, so please don't quote me to Bishop Beiler or he might put me under the Bann," Abigail went on.

Edith gave a little laugh, feeling her heavy heart lighten ever so slightly.

"But that thought also reminded me that the joy of the Lord is my strength, as Nehemiah says. Perhaps that is what we should focus on now. Let our joy be not in circumstances, but in Gott himself."

"You are the wisest maem any maedel could hope to have," Edith said gratefully.

They had reached the side door to the barn and still there was no sight nor sound of the bridegroom. Abigail stopped and turned Edith to face her. Silently, she kissed her daughter on her forehead and then nodded. Slowly, she reached out and placed her hand on the door handle.

"Are you ready, liebchen?" she queried. Edith placed her hand over her mother's.

"I don't know, Maem, maybe this is all just foolishness. Maybe I'm just being silly, like Daed said. Maybe we should just send everyone home."

A breathless silence followed as Abigail seemed to be searching for the right words to say and then a voice cut through the stillness, calling her name.

"Edie! Edie! Edie!"

Edith's fingers gripped her mother's as her head whipped toward the driveway where the sound was coming from. Her heart seemed to execute a full somersault like the ones she and Silas had loved to do when they were children on her parents' lawn. It took only a moment for her to realize that the voice belonged to the man she loved more than her own life.

He was running up the driveway toward her, discarding the blanket and the canvas bag, which were clutched in his fists, along the way. Edith didn't think twice. She took off running to meet him, not caring about her hair or her kapp or her dress. As they met, he enveloped her in his arms and lifted her feet clear off the ground as they spun round and around, laughing, with tears of joy streaming down their faces.

"I knew it!" Edie sobbed, feeling as if her grin would split her face right in two. "I knew you'd come back! I knew Gott would make a way! I just knew it!"

Silas set her down on the ground again. "And I knew you wouldn't waver. Even though I only regained my memory this morning, I knew you would be waiting. I knew you wouldn't let anyone call off our wedding," he told her breathlessly.

For a blissful, enraptured moment, they simply gazed at each other, each drinking in the sight of the other, as if to ensure they never forgot that precious moment. Then Edith started.

"Your clothes are in the guest room, ready for you!" she exclaimed excitedly. "Go get dressed, Sy! Our guests are waiting!"

As she watched him dash into the house, she hugged herself, catching her mother's eye. Entirely unbidden, the words from Proverbs rang in her spirit: *Hope deferred maketh the heart sick: but when the desire cometh, it is a tree of life.*

Epilogue
Christmas Blessings

Edith lovingly dusted off the mahogany clock with a soft cloth and replaced it on the mantelpiece. Setting down the cloth, she opened the glass door and removed the winding key, slotting it into place and turning until the loud tick-tock could be heard reverberating through the room.

She smiled and set the time correctly, then absent-mindedly traced the brass filigree corners of the face with one finger. It was still the most beautiful clock she had ever seen. For three years it had faithfully ticked off the seconds of their waiting; and suffering; and trusting. Now it was marking time to a new expectation. She felt a delicious thrill of joy run through her.

"Our trusty little Christmas clock," Silas said, wrapping his arms around her from behind and kissing her in her neck. Edith giggled. She had still not gotten used to the sensation of pure delight that her husband's touch gave her, and she hoped she never would.

"Isn't it this time last year that you were standing by the side door of your daed's barn when I came charging up the driveway?" he asked.

"Give or take a few minutes," Edith agreed. "Christmas is a truly special time for the Hauptfleisch family, isn't it?" she added coyly. "More so than for most families."

"Truer words were never spoken," Silas agreed, his voice low with affected gravity. Edith giggled again.

"Christmas is when you gave me the most beautiful clock in the world," she expounded dreamily. "And asked me to be your wife."

"And when you agreed to love nobody but me, forever and ever," Silas added, kissing her again.

"It's also when we found out what was wrong with me when I got so ill and I could start taking treatments to get better," Edith went on.

"Don't forget the next Christmas," Silas reminded her. "The one when the doctor said you were fully in remission."

Edith nodded enthusiastically. "Oh jah, I'll never forget that Christmas. But there's a better one. The one when you told me you weren't going anywhere, no matter how long it took, you would stick around, because the wedding ceremony was only the outward sign of the inner vow you had already made."

Silas drew her closer to him and held her tightly, as if he would never let her go.

"But the best one of all is when you waited, even though I wasn't there, you kept the faith, you didn't give up, and you didn't let anyone else give up, either. The day you became my wife." His voice was thick with emotion.

Edith wriggled free and turned to face her beloved. "Christmas is definitely our family's special season," she reaffirmed, but then she looked deep into Silas' eyes. "But what about the time in between?"

He didn't answer for a while and she didn't press him. She already knew what he was going to say—it was the same reply that resonated in her own heart—and yet she wanted to hear it from his lips.

"I'd say the times in between are what made it possible for us to appreciate each Christmas and its blessings," he said slowly and ruminatively. "It's what changed us enough to appreciate the Christmas blessings."

Edith's heart quivered with joy. She could not have said it better.

Silas took her face in his hands and kissed her tenderly. Then he drew away and led her to the sofa where they sat snuggled up together, still gazing at the mahogany clock and feeling the pulse of its marking time vibrate through them.

"What do you think will make *this* Christmas special for us Hauptfleischs?" Edith asked, feeling a little shudder of anticipation run through her.

Silas chuckled. "To be honest, I'd be quite happy for absolutely nothing remarkable to happen," he admitted a little sheepishly. "I've had about as many exciting Christmases as I can handle."

"You sure about that?" Edith asked teasingly.

He gave her a sidelong look. "Please tell me you're not up to something, Edith Hauptfleisch," he said with mock sternness.

"Oh, this is not something I could have done on my own," Edith assured him, feeling as if she would burst, but thoroughly enjoying stringing him along.

"So you *have* been up to something," Silas groaned dramatically, rolling his eyes. "Can't we just have *one* peaceful Christmas in our lives, please?"

"Like I said, I had help," Edith reminded him.

"Alright, enough with your riddles already." Silas chuckled and reclined against the backrest of the sofa. "We've been married for a full year already and I still haven't solved even one of them."

Edith sat up straight and looked into his eyes. "Can you keep a secret, Sy?" she asked, making a serious face.

"Probably not as well as you can, but I can try," Silas responded evasively.

"Trying won't be good enough. This is a secret you can tell *nobody*, not even my Maem or Daed, not even *your* Maem or Daed …" she let her voice trail off. Her words were having the desired effect if the look on Silas's face was anything to go by.

His eyes grew wide as saucers and his jaw grew slack as he held her gaze in disbelief.

"Are you saying what I think you're saying, Edie?" he queried.

"If you're asking if I'm telling you we'll have to pick out baby names, then jah, that's what I'm telling you."

Silas stared at her wordlessly. "But I thought …" he began and seemed unable to finish.

"Jah, Dr. Graham said chemotherapy could affect our ability to conceive, even years after my treatment, but I don't think Gott bothers with what doctors say." Edith smiled at him, happiness washing over her in wave after blissful wave. Silas looked worried.

"He also said …" he began and stopped in mid-sentence once more.

"I know," Edith reassured him. "He also said any pregnancy I had could end prematurely."

"We could lose our baby," Silas spelled out the awful facts, his eyes haunted. "I prayed we would be spared such a loss, Edie. I prayed *you* would be spared such a loss. You've been through so much already …" Silas's voice broke.

"And after all *we've* been through, Sy, should we not be trusting that Gott can give us another miracle?"

Silas sat up straight. "I almost feel like we've had our quota. Why would he shower so many on us?"

"Because it's His plan," Edith said simply. "I believe nothing Gott does is only for one person. This baby is not only ours, but His. He already has a life planned out for him or her. A life that will change other lives and give Him glory if we are faithful to raise him or her in Gott's ways."

"Even if he or she doesn't make it out into the world?" Silas asked tremulously. Edith nodded, loving him for his compassion.

"Even then," she affirmed.

Silas nodded slowly. Then he gathered Edith back into his arms and held her close against his chest. She could feel his heart beating as his warmth seeped into her.

"Then I will do everything in my power to protect both of you," Silas declared, his voice full of firm determination.

"I know," Edith said and lifted her face to his.

"Just like you knew I would come back from Cabbage Hill on our wedding day."

Edith reached up her hands and drew his head closer. They kissed tenderly and deeply, neither of them needing to answer that question out loud.

*** The End ***

Thank you kindly for choosing to read my book. I sincerely hope you enjoyed it. All of my Amish Romances are wholesome stories suitable for all to enjoy.

If you could be so kind to leave a review on Amazon, I would appreciate it.